Dear Parent:
Your child's love of reading starts here!

Every child learns to read in a different way and at his or her own speed. Some go back and forth between reading levels and read favorite books again and again. Others read through each level in order. You can help your young reader improve and become more confident by encouraging his or her own interests and abilities. From books your child reads with you to the first books he or she reads alone, there are I Can Read Books for every stage of reading:

SHARED READING
Basic language, word repetition, and whimsical illustrations, ideal for sharing with your emergent reader

BEGINNING READING
Short sentences, familiar words, and simple concepts for children eager to read on their own

READING WITH HELP
Engaging stories, longer sentences, and language play for developing readers

READING ALONE
Complex plots, challenging vocabulary, and high-interest topics for the independent reader

ADVANCED READING
Short paragraphs, chapters, and exciting themes for the perfect bridge to chapter books

I Can Read Books have introduced children to the joy of reading since 1957. Featuring award-winning authors and illustrators and a fabulous cast of beloved characters, I Can Read Books set the standard for beginning readers.

A lifetime of discovery begins with the magical words **"I Can Read!"**

Visit www.icanread.com for information
on enriching your child's reading experience.

For Ritchie Garcia and his class of second graders
—J.O'C.

For the children of Tarbut V'Torah: some of the future
caretakers of our beautiful Earth
—R.P.G.

For two sisters, Audrey and Kaelan, who take good care
of the Earth
—A.I. and O.I.

I Can Read Book® is a trademark of HarperCollins Publishers.

Library of Congress Cataloging-in-Publication Data
O'Connor, Jane.
     Every day is Earth Day / by Jane O'Connor ; cover illustration by Robin Preiss Glasser ; interior illustrations by Aleksey Ivanov and Olga Ivanov. — 1st ed.
        p.   cm. — (Fancy Nancy) (I can read! Level 1)
     Summary: When Nancy, the girl who loves to use fancy words, learns about Earth Day and "being green," her enthusiasm causes problems at home.
     ISBN 978-0-06-187327-0 (trade bdg.) — ISBN 978-0-06-187326-3 (pbk.)
     [1. Earth Day—Fiction.   2. Environmental protection—Fiction.   3. Family life—Fiction.   4. Schools—Fiction.
5. Vocabulary—Fiction.]   I. Ivanov, A. (Aleksey), ill.   II. Ivanov, O. (Olga), ill.   III. Title.
PZ7.O222Eve   2010   2009014585
[E]—dc22   CIP
                                                                                                                                                   AC

10 11 12 13 14   LP/WOR   10 9 8 7 6 5 4 3 2 1   ❖   First Edition

I Can Read!

BEGINNING 1 READING

Fancy NANCY

Every Day
Is Earth Day

by Jane O'Connor

cover illustration by Robin Preiss Glasser

interior illustrations by
Aleksey Ivanov and Olga Ivanov

HARPER

An Imprint of HarperCollinsPublishers

I do not like the color green
very much.

You can tell by my crayons.

The green one looks almost new.

But I adore being green.
(Adore is fancy for
really, really loving something.)
Being green means taking care
of our planet.

Ms. Glass asks,

"Who can tell us about Earth Day?"

I wave my hand and say,

"It is like a holiday for our planet."

"That's right," says Ms. Glass.
"But I like to think that
every day is Earth Day."

Our class discusses rules

for being green.

(Discuss means to talk—

only it's fancier and more serious.)

Then we write the rules down.

At home I am shocked!

I see that my family needs

to be much greener.

My dad is about to drive

to the supermarket.

"Dad," I say,

"the green rule is:

Less than a mile?

Then bike in style."

At the checkout line

the guy asks my dad

if we want paper or plastic bags.

I say to my dad,

"Please take note.

Always bring a tote."

(Tote is a fancy word for shopping bag.)

Later that night it gets cold.

My mom wants to turn up the heat.

"No, Mom," I say.

"It's better to wear a sweater."

14

In the morning

I stand outside the bathroom.

Very soon I shout,

"Dad, don't waste water.

Get clean, but stay green."

At school we each make a poster.

Robert says,

"We are like superheroes.

We are protecting planet Earth."

That night

I see that my mom's computer is on.

Right away, I turn it off.

My mom comes into the room.

She sees the blank screen.

"Why did you do that?" she asks.

I tell her she is wasting energy.

"I was writing something for work,"
my mom says.

"I just went to get my glasses.

Now I lost everything I wrote.

I have to start all over!"

She is very irritated.

(That is fancy for mad.)

But how was I to know?

I am just protecting the planet.

I tell my sister not to run water

while she brushes her teeth.

I remind my parents

to turn off lights in empty rooms.

Before bed

I go into my sister's room.

I start to turn off her lamp.

"Oh no!" my mom says.

"Your sister is afraid of the dark.

She likes the light on."

Soon my sister is asleep.

Now she does not need the light on.

I tiptoe into her room

and turn off her light.

In the middle of the night

I wake up.

I hear my sister crying.

What is wrong?

"Your sister woke up
and got scared," Dad says.
"She was alone in the dark.
Did you turn off her lamp?"

"Yes," I say. "I am so sorry.

I didn't think she would wake up."

I start crying too.

The next morning my parents say,

"It is important to be green.

And we will try harder.

But you must not be so bossy.

And you must be flexible."

(That is the opposite of stubborn.)

At school I perk up.

Ms. Glass adores my poster.

(My green crayon does not look

new anymore.)

My family really is greener now.

Tonight at dinner

we use candles, not lightbulbs.

We use cloth napkins, not paper ones.

Guess what!
Being green can also
be very fancy.

Fancy Nancy's Fancy Words

These are the fancy words in this book:

Adore—to really, really love something or someone

Discuss—to talk seriously

Flexible—the opposite of stubborn

Irritated—mad

Tote—a shopping bag

Here's what Nancy learned:

Less than a mile? Then bike in style.

Please take note. Always bring a tote.

In cold weather, keep the room temperature low. It's better to wear a sweater.

Don't waste water. Get clean, but stay green.